Learning to Read, Step by Step!

Ready to Read   Preschool–Kindergarten
• big type and easy words • rhyme and rhythm • picture clues
For children who know the alphabet and are eager to begin reading.

Reading with Help   Preschool–Grade 1
• basic vocabulary • short sentences • simple stories
For children who recognize familiar words and sound out new words with help.

Reading on Your Own   Grades 1–3
• engaging characters • easy-to-follow plots • popular topics
For children who are ready to read on their own.

Reading Paragraphs   Grades 2–3
• challenging vocabulary • short paragraphs • exciting stories
For newly independent readers who read simple sentences with confidence.

Ready for Chapters   Grades 2–4
• chapters • longer paragraphs • full-color art
For children who want to take the plunge into chapter books but still like colorful pictures.

STEP INTO READING® is designed to give every child a successful reading experience. The grade levels are only guides; children will progress through the steps at their own speed, developing confidence in their reading. The F&P Text Level on the back cover serves as another tool to help you choose the right book for your child.

Remember, a lifetime love of reading starts with a single step!

Text copyright © 1988 by Random House, Inc. Illustrations copyright © 1988 by Michael Eagle. All rights reserved. Published in the United States by Random House Children's Books, a division of Random House LLC, a Penguin Random House Company, New York.

Step into Reading, Random House, and the Random House colophon are registered trademarks of Random House LLC.

Visit us on the Web!
StepIntoReading.com
randomhouse.com/kids

Educators and librarians, for a variety of teaching tools, visit us at
RHTeachersLibrarians.com

Library of Congress Cataloging-in-Publication Data
Little, Emily.
The Trojan horse : how the Greeks won the war / by Emily Little ; illustrated by Michael Eagle.
p. cm. — (Step into reading. A step 5 book.)
Summary: Recounts how the Greeks used a wooden horse to win the Trojan War.
ISBN 978-0-394-89674-8 (trade) — ISBN 978-0-385-39074-3 (lib. bdg.)
1. Trojan horse (Greek mythology)—Juvenile literature. [1. Trojan War. 2. Mythology, Greek.]
I. Eagle, Michael, ill. II. Title. III. Series: Step into reading. Step 5 book.
BL820.T75L58 2003 398.2'0938'02—dc21 2002013675

Printed in the United States of America
50 49 48 47 46 45 44 43 42 41

This book has been officially leveled by using the F&P Text Level Gradient™ Leveling System.

STEP INTO READING®

A HISTORY READER

THE TROJAN HORSE

How the Greeks Won the War

by Emily Little
illustrated by Michael Eagle

Random House 🏠 New York

1
The Wall

It is three thousand years ago in the land now called Turkey. A shepherd stands above a grassy field, watching his sheep. To the west the sea sparkles in the sunlight. To the east the dusty plain stirs in the wind.

About four miles from the sea there is a great stone wall built on a hill. Inside the wall there is a rich, proud kingdom.

It is the ancient kingdom of Troy.

The wall around Troy is there to protect the city. It is made of stones that men cut and fit together. In some places it is very high and very thick. The lower part of the wall is covered with limestone. The limestone makes the wall slippery. Climbing up the wall is impossible.

At the top of the wall there are places where the Trojan bowmen can stand. Here they can pull back their bowstrings and let their arrows fly. So going over the wall is impossible too!

There is only one way into Troy—through the great double gate. Shepherds go through, with their bundles of wool. Plowmen go through, with their carts full of vegetables. Traders go through, with their treasures of gold and silver and bronze.

Gatekeepers guard the gate day and night.
If a hostile army is coming across the plain,
they close the gate and push in the bolts.
Behind the bolted gate, behind the stone wall,
Troy is safe.

Troy is an important city in the ancient world. And Priam,* the king of Troy, is a very powerful ruler. He has many allies. He rules the land and sea for miles around. But King Priam is not content. He wants to be more powerful than the Greeks, who live far away across the Aegean Sea.

The Greeks speak the same language as the Trojans and believe in the same gods as the Trojans. But they are enemies, not friends!

The land where the Greeks live is rocky and hilly. They cannot grow enough wheat. They must sail to Asia to buy more. But to get to Asia the Greeks must pass through a narrow channel of water that connects the Aegean Sea with the Black Sea. Troy is located at the very entrance to this channel.

King Priam takes advantage of this! When a Greek ship full of cargo sails past Troy, the Trojans stop it. They demand a toll. If the Greeks want to go by, they must pay!

*A pronunciation guide can be found on page 48.

Cargo ships are big and heavy. They are not made to go fast like warships. So the Greeks have to pay the toll—with bags of wheat, jars of oil, bars of gold.

The Greeks are furious. Why should they have to pay to use the channel? The sea is free. If the Trojans keep this up, there will be war!

But King Priam is not afraid. There is a great stone wall around his city. No one—not even a Greek army—can get into Troy.

2
War!

In the Greek kingdom of Sparta, King Menelaus paces the floor and plans his revenge. Something terrible has happened. The Trojans have captured his wife, Helen. They have taken her to Troy.

Helen! She is the most beautiful woman in the world. And now she will be forced to marry Paris, prince of Troy!

Menelaus plans to go to Troy with his army.

But he cannot fight alone. The Trojans and their allies outnumber the Spartans.

Menelaus summons a runner. He gives him a message to take to his brother, Agamemnon.

In the Greek kingdom of Mycenae, King Agamemnon sits and listens. A runner has brought him a message. The Trojans have taken Helen!

Troy! That city has been pirating Greek ships for years. This kidnapping is the final straw! Greece must act. The Greek armies must band together. The time has come to make war.

Agamemnon goes to the temple to pray. He bows before the sacred statue of Athena, goddess of war, goddess of wisdom. He asks for help. He has his men place a giant bull at the feet of the statue. If Athena likes this gift, she will side with the Greeks.

In the Greek kingdom of Ithaca the king's son Odysseus is saying good-bye to his wife and son. He is going to Troy. The Greek armies are banding together to fight the Trojans, and they need a strong, shrewd leader like Odysseus.

The warships are loaded. Everything is on board—armor, weapons, chariots, food, even horses! The sail is up. The oarsmen are ready to row.

Odysseus stays a minute longer. His son is just a baby. He promises to return as soon as he can.

As the Greeks sail toward Troy, Trojan scouts bring the news to Priam.

The Greeks are coming!

Priam goes to the temple to pray. He bows before the sacred statue of Athena, goddess of war, goddess of wisdom. He asks for help. He has his men place a giant ram at the feet of the statue. If Athena likes this gift, she will side with the Trojans.

In the palace nearby, Helen sits by a window and watches the sea. The jewels in her gold crown sparkle in the sunlight.

Suddenly she sees something on the horizon. A ship! Two ships! More ships than she can count!

The Greeks are coming!

The Greek ships land on the sandy beach near Troy. Odysseus leads his army east—horses, chariots, and all!

The bowmen go on foot, with their bows and arrows. The spearmen walk behind, side by side, with their shields and long spears. The bravest, most skilled warriors ride in the chariots. Their swords dangle at their sides. The Greek army is ready for battle.

The Trojan gate opens. The men of Troy come out. They are ready for battle too. King Priam leads his army west across the plain—horses, chariots, and all!

The Trojans and the Greeks meet on the flat, rocky fields between the city and the sea.

The fighting begins. The bowmen take aim on either side and let their arrows fly. The spearmen shake their spears and hurl them at each other. The chariots race around the battlefield. The Greeks chase the Trojans. The Trojans chase the Greeks. Warriors leap from their chariots to fight with their swords.

Arrows zing. Spears clang. Horses' hooves pound the ground. Dust fills the air. Many are wounded. Many are killed.

But when the battle is over, no one has won. The Trojans go back to their city. The Greeks go back to the shore and build their camp near a river. Both sides get ready for the next battle.

The fighting continues—day after day, week after week, month after month. Both sides are equally skilled. As long as the war is fought on the battlefield, no one can win.

Odysseus realizes that there is only one way for the Greeks to defeat Troy—they must get *inside* the city.

But how?

3
The Horse

Ten years go by—ten long years! The Trojan war is still going on.

The Greeks are tired—tired of fighting, tired of living in huts, tired of being away from home. Odysseus's men sit by the campfire and argue. Some want to return to Greece. Others refuse to surrender. The men say that the Greeks must give Athena a bigger gift. Then she will side with the Greeks at last.

Odysseus looks out to sea. He notices the ships floating in the water. No one builds ships as well as the Greeks. The Greeks can build anything!

Suddenly Odysseus thinks of a way to get inside Troy—a way to win the war. It is an extraordinary plan.

Odysseus tells Agamemnon about his idea. The plan is dangerous. If it fails, many Greeks will be killed. But if it succeeds, Troy will fall. Agamemnon agrees to take the risk. So do the other kings.

Some ships are sent to the nearest Greek islands. There the men cut down many trees and put them on board. When the ships return with their cargo, Odysseus tells his best carpenters what to do.

The men cut the trees into logs, the logs into planks, and some of the planks into strips. Then they build a giant wooden frame. It is very tall, perhaps even taller than the Trojan wall!

The men weave the strips of wood around and through the frame. The construction begins to look like a horse—a giant wooden horse! The horse is hollow. There is a door on the side just big enough for a man to crawl through.

When the horse is finished, Odysseus and his men go up a rope and drop down into the belly of the horse. The men are wearing their armor. They are carrying their weapons.

When the horse is full of men, the door on the side is closed.

The rest of the Greeks board the ships and sail away. They take with them their food, their horses, their chariots. Only one man stays behind. His name is Sinon. He goes to hide in the grass by the river.

There is an island not far from the shore. The Greek ships sail past the island and stop on the other side—out of sight! The island is deserted. No one sees the Greek ships hiding in the bay.

A lookout goes ashore. He climbs to the top of a hill. From there he can see the wall around Troy.

A plowman runs along the old cart road toward the Trojan gate. He is shouting wonderful news.

The Greeks are gone!

Soon the great double gate is opened. Soon the people of Troy come crowding out.

The war is over!

The Trojan people walk all the way down to the Greek camp. They want to see the empty huts. They want to see the deserted stable.

The Trojans cannot believe their eyes. There stands a giant wooden horse! What can it be? Why did the Greeks leave it in their camp?

4
Doom Is Near!

The crowd around the horse grows bigger and bigger. The Trojans are suspicious. Everyone is talking at once. Inside the horse's wooden belly, the Greeks can hear what the Trojans are saying.

Burn the Greek horse! Chop it to pieces! Push it into the sea!

King Priam arrives. He, too, is suspicious. He tells his men to examine the horse.

Suddenly there is shouting from the river. Trojan scouts have found something—someone! It is a man, a Greek! They found him hiding in the grass.

Sinon is brought before the king. The people want to kill him. He is a Greek! But King Priam stops them. Here is someone who can tell them what the horse means. He demands an explanation.

Every eye is on Sinon as he speaks. He tells the king that he ran away because the Greeks were about to kill him for disobeying orders. Sinon lies and everyone believes him.

But what about the horse?

Sinon says that the wooden horse is a gift for Athena. Now Athena will give the Greeks a safe trip home.

King Priam is worried. If the Trojans destroy the horse, Athena will be angry. So he commands his men to bring the horse into Troy. The Trojans will give the horse to Athena instead.

The Trojans place a giant slab of rock under the horse. They place logs with wheels under the slab. They throw ropes around the horse's neck. It takes many men and many oxen to drag the giant horse across the old battlefield all the way to Troy.

As the horse rolls along, the Greeks inside bump against each other. Their weapons and armor clatter together, but no one hears.

Outside there is too much cheering.

At the Trojan gate there is trouble. The horse is too big. The Trojans have to tear down many stones to make way for the horse.

The Trojan people shout. Let the horse come into the city! The wooden horse goes through the great double gate.

At last! The Greeks are inside Troy!

The horse is pulled along the streets—past the marketplace, past the houses, past the palace—all the way to the temple of Athena.

Now there is a great festival in Athena's honor. Everyone in Troy celebrates. They sing and dance in the streets. They drink and feast far into the night. The priestesses burn incense in the temple and chant their special prayers to her. All of them thank the goddess for ending the war.

All but one! The young priestess named
Cassandra is troubled. She walks like a phan-
tom through the streets, crying out. Doom is
near! Doom is near!

No one pays any attention.

5

The Fall

The night sky is full of stars. Troy sleeps. Everyone is full of food and wine. Everyone except the Greek warriors inside the Trojan horse! A crack appears in the side of the horse. A door is opened. A rope is dropped. Down the rope come Odysseus and his men.

Some go to the top of the wall. They kill the guards. One Greek lights a torch. Far away on an island a lookout sees the signal.

The Greek ships sail back to Troy. The men cross the plain in the dark of night. They enter Troy at the gate through the hole the Trojans made.

Suddenly there is shouting. The Greeks
run through the streets, carrying torches.
They set fires everywhere.

The people wake up. Their houses are full
of smoke. They run outside to see what is
happening.

The Trojan warriors wake up too. They are sleepy from too much food and wine. They stumble about, looking for their swords.

In the palace King Priam wakes up. The guards are shouting the news outside his chamber door. The Greeks are inside the city!

Now Priam knows the truth. Troy has been tricked!

Troy burns. Everything that is not made of stone goes up in flames. The heat is intense. There is not enough water in all of Troy to put out even one blaze.

Some of the Trojans run out of the city. They escape by land and by sea. But many die in the fire.

The fire burns for three days. When it is out, the rich, proud kingdom of Troy is gone.

After the fall of Troy, the Greeks go home. Menelaus takes Helen back to Sparta.

Agamemnon returns to Mycenae. But clever Odysseus is not so lucky. He is captured on his way home, and it takes him ten more years to get back to Ithaca, back to his wife and his son.

Many years go by. The ruins of Troy lie inside the great stone wall. The wind blows the dust across the plain and across the ruins. The stones are buried in the dust.

6

Discovery

It is the 700s B.C., about four hundred years after the Trojan war.

A Greek poet named Homer decides to write down the stories he has heard about the war. There are so many and everyone in Greece loves to hear them. In his long poem Homer tells about the heroes of the war—Odysseus, Agamemnon, Menelaus, and many others. He describes the battles on the plain outside

Troy. He writes about Helen and the goddess Athena. His long poem about the Trojan war is called the *Iliad.*

More than two thousand years later a German archaeologist named Heinrich Schliemann reads the *Iliad.* It is the oldest piece of Greek writing that still exists. By now all traces of Troy have disappeared. Many people think that Homer made up the story. But Schliemann believes that there really was a city called Troy, and he decides to find it.

Schliemann goes to Turkey. From clues in the *Iliad,* he locates the hill where Troy was probably built. To the west the sea sparkles in the sunlight. To the east the dusty plain stirs in the wind.

In 1870 Schliemann begins digging. Many people laugh at him. But Schliemann believes he will find Troy...and he does!

He not only discovers the great stone wall, he finds many other things too—treasures of silver and gold and bronze. He finds human

skeletons and the bones of horses. He finds
a gold crown.

Troy did exist! The war that Homer wrote
about was real!

But there are many things that Schliemann
does not find—the statue of Athena, the chariots, the wooden horse. These things are gone
forever.

But the story of the wooden horse—handed
down for three thousand years—remains!

Pronunciation Guide

Here are phonetic spellings of the difficult names in this book.

Aegean Sea   [ih-JEE-un see]
Agamemnon   [ag-uh-MEM-non]
Athena   [uh-THEE-nuh]
Heinrich Schliemann   [HINE-rick SHLEE-man]
Iliad   [ILL-ee-ud]
Ithaca   [ITH-uh-kuh]
Menelaus   [men-uh-LAY-us]
Mycenae   [my-SEE-nee]
Odysseus   [oh-DIS-ee-us]
Priam   [PRY-um]
Sinon   [SY-non]

No one knows the whole story of the Trojan War. This book is based on the legends of Homer and Virgil, as well as on accounts by modern historians.

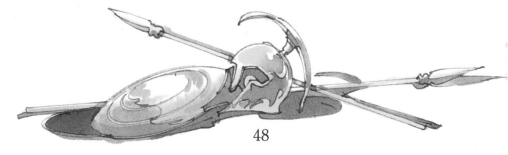